One Hungry Baby

With much love for A.J.C. and P.E.C.,
who led the way.
For R.J.O., who gave me the time.
And for Archie,
my very own hungry baby.
L.M.O.

Text copyright © 1992 by Lucy Coats
Illustrations copyright © 1992 by Sue Hellard

Published by Crown Publishers, Inc., a Random House company, 201 East 50th Street,
New York, New York 10022. First published in Great Britain in 1992 by Orchard Books.
CROWN is a trademark of Crown Publishers, Inc.
Manufactured in Italy

Library of Congress Cataloging-in-Publication Data
Coats, Lucy.
One hungry baby : a bedtime counting rhyme / rhyme by Lucy Coats; pictures by Sue Hellard.
p. cm.
Summary: Ten animal babies perform various activities before bed, including eating, bathing,
and listening to stories.
[1. Bedtime—Fiction. 2. Babies—Fiction. 3. Animals—Fiction. 4. Counting. 5. Stories in rhyme.]
I. Hellard, Susan, ill. II. Title.
PZ8.3.C595On   1994
[E]—dc20   93-42620
ISBN 0-517-59887-6

10 9 8 7 6 5 4 3 2 1

First American Edition

One Hungry Baby

A BEDTIME COUNTING RHYME

by LUCY COATS

pictures by SUE HELLARD

CROWN PUBLISHERS, INC., New York

One hungry baby,

Two front teeth,

Three dribbly chins
With bibs underneath.

Four bubbly bathtimes
To wash off the crumbs.

Five sploshy splashers,

Five wet moms.

Six funny dads
Drying six button noses.

Seven big sisters
Counting tails and toeses.

Eight fat teddies

Ready for bed.

Nine soft pillows,
Nine sleepy heads.

Ten good babies
Tucked up tight.

Twenty tired parents
Waving good night.